TRUMPETER
The Story of a Swan

TRUMPETER
The Story of a Swan

by

Jane and Paul Annixter

illustrated by
Gilbert Riswold

HOLIDAY HOUSE • NEW YORK

Library of Congress Cataloging in Publication Data

Annixter, Jane, pseud.
Trumpeter, the story of a swan.

SUMMARY: The adventures of a trumpeter swan and his
flock as they migrate each winter from their Arctic
home to the Louisiana swamps.
1. Trumpeter swan—Juvenile literature.
[1. Trumpeter swan. 2. Swans] I. Annixter, Paul,
pseud., joint author. II. Riswold, Gilbert, illus.
III. Title.
QL696.A52A55   598.4′1   73-76796
ISBN 0-8234-0227-4

FOR BETH AND ANN

CHAPTER ONE

Arctic Spring

Spring's beginnings were a tearing wind from the north that scarred the face of the remaining snow. There were high-pitched crescendos of sound from the nearby sea as ice floe ground against ice floe or some great ice pan was forced over the surface of another. It was a treeless land lying far up near the roof of the world where the great Barren Ground stretched northward through unbroken desolation towards the Pole.

For a time in this north world winter seemed to be holding its own. Where the snow was thin the low flat tundra was brown and dead. But abruptly a kind of soft puffing began from the southwest. It lasted through two long days and suddenly, dramatically routed the last forces of winter. The reaches of sphagnum moss began to turn faintly green. A few lemmings came out of their holes. An Arctic hare appeared with patches of dun gray in his winter white coat.

Migratory birds began to arrive: Canada geese breaking from their orderly Vs to descend, ducks of many tribes wheeling and settling on the waters. Soon legions of ivory and black backed gulls were coming in, and pirate skuas, and jaegers, and many others.

Though all the migrants had traveled the skies for thousands of miles, rest and recovery seemed simultaneous with their arrival here. High-pitched excitement took them, flock by flock. Everywhere the clamor of bird voices covered the land as the migrants went about the great spring business of choosing mates and building nests. Birds!—flying, swimming, diving, quarreling, feeding, and courting, with an abandon that came only where hunters never stalked and where the days were twenty-two hours long, the season of the midnight sun.

Toward the end of one of those almost endless spring days, in the hour when the light was changing from apple green to turquoise and the low southwest welled deepest color, horn notes suddenly filled the air. Out of high sky appeared a ragged line of great white swans. Their eight-foot wing spread made them appear larger than life and their breasts caught the changing light in flashes of crimson and sapphire. As they circled to come in their trumpeting blared forth like clarion calls announcing royalty.

There were hoarse deep signals from the flock leaders as the birds tipped majestically earthward, winding down to water as if along some invisible spiral stairway. The trumpeters alighted with perfect control, wing tips turned down, their black webbed feet thrust out before them as they skied to a stop.

In the lake waters roundabout a strange thing happened: there was a pause like a held breath; all babble of the flocks had ceased. Then, as if in homage to these monarchs of the air, every bird for hundreds of yards around sprang upward in unison and slowly settled again.

There were some thirty birds in this trumpeter flock, a third fewer than had left the wintering place in the marshes of Louisiana. All along the flyways hunters had been waiting, and many of the noble birds had fallen. Back in the early 1800s, before the fur trade learned the commercial value of swan products, there had been countless Vs and strings of trumpeter swans moving up to the Arctic each spring, and back south again in the autumn to Texas, Louisiana, and Mexico. But the uses for swansdown increased—quilts, featherbeds, powder puffs. So along the flyways hunters were always waiting, and every migratory flight took great toll.

Only the hardiest of the flocks still made the long semiannual passage. But here in the northland the century-long persecution was forgotten. They had come through one more time, and this was safe harbor in a true bird world.

The swans rode high on the water like large white liners among a lot of harbor tugs. About them was none of the clamorous excitement and hurry shown by the other birds. Now and again exchanging horn notes, they stretched their long necks and preened their snowy feathers. The younger birds swam to the shallows to feed on pond weeds and tubers. The elders, including an especially regal pair who floated with flight quills touching, simply rested and collected themselves. There were no single flight leaders among the trumpeters, but the magnificent cob resting with his mate had done his share of guiding the flock to this Arctic nesting ground. His proud head rose inches above others of his kind; his black bill was corrugated from long use as a weapon of defense. The pen, his graceful mate, had a mild look in contrast to the electric spark of dominance and courage in the cob's black eye.

Jewel colors lingered in the low sky. The lake still held a subdued light, but semidarkness had descended over the tundra. The pair slept now, still close together, with necks curved back and bills resting between their wings.

The waterfowl talk continued through the short night. Awake again, the cob and his mate sailed about in the limited space between rafts of ducks and geese. The swans were hemmed in even more when a flock of cranes arrived with loud croakings that jarred the air. The immemorial image that the trumpeters carried was of vast spaces awaiting them here. In the past they had been the first to arrive, but often now they had to hide by day and fly only at night to avoid passages where hunters habitually lay in wait. As they moved the smaller birds made respectful way for them, but there was scarcely enough room to stretch their wide wings and air their feathers in the fresh flow of wind from the south.

The two preened with care, then made their way to the shallows to feed on the succulent roots and tubers near the margin of the lake. Swans could not dive for food as the ducks did but would reach for what they wanted, stretching their long necks, beaks exploring the shallows and tails in the air.

During the long day the lake waters gradually cleared. The smaller migrants paired off and sought their nesting places in the surrounding muskeg. Geese were the first to remove themselves. The pintails and mergansers and brants gabbled on; then these, too, began to leave the water. Family after family swam ashore and waddled to their chosen places. Now the trumpeters had room for their easy running take-offs and long sliding stops. It was a swan lake again, and that evening in the jewel-colored light their trumpetings rose to a happy crescendo that carried for a mile or more over the desolate tundra.

After a time the swans, too, sought their old nesting places. Here and there on the banks along the waterways were the remains of mounds, like watchtowers made of mud and sticks, all that remained of the trumpeters' nests after the winter storms. These stood out boldly, in full view of every marauder of the waste, for trumpeters did not hide their homes but relied upon themselves to protect their young.

The kingly cob and his mate rediscovered their own special site on a spit of land among interlocking waterways. The nest itself had been battered to the ground. They would have to collect fresh material and build again, but this did not disturb them. The pen stood quietly waiting on the pile of loose sticks and dry grasses that had held her eggs of the year before, while her mate moved about inspecting the area for a possible fox hole or other signs of predators. Satisfied that all was well he returned to her carrying in his bill a stout reed which he dropped on the old stick pile.

Together they added a few more pieces of building material, but there was no hurry. In the nearby shallows they found ample aquatic growth to support a family. Later there would be yellow pond lilies blooming round

about and edible water-shield too. None would dispute
their right to this narrow point of land. Any attempt to
nest close by would be disputed hotly. Even now, with
no nest to protect, the cob was on guard. When a large
gyrfalcon swooped low overhead, the trumpeter hissed
fiercely, his long neck stretched toward the enemy, bill
snapping. This bugling challenge was the loudest, most
imperious sound made by any bird. The white gyr
whipped upward, then circled to stare down, as if to fix
in mind the identity of this defiant one.

When the interloper was gone, the cob flexed and
then closed his wide white wings before entering the
water. The pen followed, floating serenely at his side.

The swans' nest building filled a number of long bril-
liant days. The completed tower commanded a broad
view. No creature could approach without being seen and
quickly driven off. Now the first egg was laid, buff gray in
color and about twice the size of a hen's egg. Each morning for four days an additional egg was laid, and the pen
began her long brooding.

Though weeks must pass before there would be the
first faint sounds within the shells, she already seemed to
be listening, head bent, perfectly absorbed and content.
The cob was constantly on guard. He had extended his
patrol to cover an acre or so. Not even a swan relative
was allowed within twenty yards of the nest. Once when
a rustling sound was heard he went bugling into the
muskeg, neck thrust forward, bill snapping. But it was
only a water vole which had momentarily popped from
its hole and popped right back again.

On a beautiful sunny morning five weeks after the

first egg was laid, the mother swan heard tiny tappings in one of the five warm eggs beneath her breast. The cob drew nearer, listening as intently as his mate. These were the sounds of new life for which they had both waited so long—"egg-teeth," sharp points at the tip of the bill, were at work within the shells.

By now on the green-tinged expanse of tundra there were many low-growing blooms. Pink saxifrage came first; trillium and orange lousewort dotted the flat places. Arctic willows, scarcely more than six inches high, were unrolling their tiny leaves, minute silvery catkins already swelling on their low branches.

Toward midday, after long and ordered rapping, the first nestling broke through. Thrusting his shell aside like the lid of a box he struggled forth all bare and damp against his mother's breast. *Olor*. His name meant "all white," but he would have to grow into it, for his first coat of down was grayish in color. His neck at this point was no longer than a gosling's.

In the next few hours Olor's two brothers and two sisters emerged from their shells, and the mother swan was half standing in the nest to give the sprawlers some room. The proud father spread the news with mighty trumpetings, then strode about shaking his wings like banners.

CHAPTER TWO

Olor

There was a twenty-four-hour period of warming and drying out; then the five little cygnets trooped down to the lake after their mother and followed her right in. They needed no swimming lessons—water was for them. They were buoyant as little corks.

The cob helped feed the family. At first the cygnets' diet was insects, but after a while they were watching their parents reach underwater for tubers and stems and trying to do it too. Their mother showed them the tender white parts of sedges and how to tip-tilt their bottoms at the margin of the lake and scoop up billfuls of mud and sieve them for the fleshy stems. When they succeeded in this she praised them. When they strayed from the nursery school limits of the lake she called them back.

One day while they were still no more than duck size, a gray white arrow came hissing earthward from mid-sky to strike directly into the clustered cygnets. The gyr-falcon had unerringly marked his prey from high above, and before the mother could come to their defense one of her young had been blasted from life in a small explosion of feathers. The gyrfalcon swept upward again with a soft broken form dangling from his talons.

When the time came for flying lessons the mother swan took off with a beautiful splash and clatter and then called to her young from the air. She repeated this maneuver until the cygnets fluttered and struggled along the surface of the water and finally lifted a few inches before falling back again with sharp disappointed cries. Olor was the biggest and strongest, and he tried the hardest, bouncing and flapping, fighting the water with his webbed feet. Sometimes his mother turned in her flight to cheer him on. Over and over in the course of a long day the parent birds would skim low over the water with encouraging calls, and the cygnets would blunder after them.

Suddenly and wonderfully one morning Olor was in the air. Not for long or very far, but airborne he was, and it was a great feeling. Finding himself back in the water he had to try again right away. And this went on and on.

What Olor's brother and sisters could not learn fast enough by watching their parents, they quickly learned from him. Here was one of them doing it. The other three hopped and skittered with renewed confidence and one by one took off for a brief glide. There were many long days of practice, but they were getting better all the time and their wings were strengthening with use. The first time all four cygnets were airborne at the same moment, proud trumpetings sounded from above and both parent birds joined the new little flock.

Now there were higher longer flights and more complicated maneuvers. Between lessons the family swam together on foraging expeditions. Like their parents, the cygnets had become vegetarians, craving only green stems, tender bulbs, and various roots to be grasped with the bill and pulled out of the shallows. In each twenty-two-hour day there was a great inflow of solar energy and many extra meals. The cygnets were nearly full size now, though their necks still had inches to grow and their beaks were still pale.

For the older pair the time of molting flight feathers arrived. For one lunar month they would be grounded, their flying limited to skimmings over the water. The cygnets learned to heed their signals, following across moss and sedge to nearby flashets, but for them flying practice went on.

There was new fun in being on their own, especially with a precocious brother to lead the way. Gabbling with excitement, Olor flapped into the eye of the wind, then volplaned back in a wide arc, imitating his sire's peremptory call, while his three siblings followed suit. His aerial confidence steadily increased. Whatever the weather, he was up there trying his wings in the wind, and often his calls were answered by exasperated trumpetings from his grounded parents.

When the other cygnets found his aeronautics too strenuous, Olor flew alone, but his brother tried to emulate him and their two sisters did their best to fly with them. One gusty afternoon in August all four were trying the air currents while their parents looked on from below. Soon out-maneuvered, the sisters went fluttering back. Now Olor left his brother behind, but the weaker cygnet persisted and was presently caught in a fierce updraft. Swept out of familiar range, he plummeted into a patch of swamp where a number of large predatory gulls called skuas were busily harassing some ivory gulls. The skuas' object was to scare the gulls into disgorging their recent catch, thus saving them the trouble of fishing for themselves. But the wind-battered cygnet was more immediate prey, and with beak and claw the skuas closed in upon him.

Planing higher, Olor had escaped the freak blast and the fate of his brother. From below, the cob had seen that one of his young had been swept out of range. When faint rapacious cries reached the parental ear, the cob flung toward the sounds. Moments later he was in the midst of the flapping, tearing predators. He was too late to save his luckless offspring, but with his great wings he beat off the attackers, shaking one of them to death in steel-like mandibles. Trumpeting his wrath he reared above the crumpled but still breathing form of his young.

The skuas scattered respectfully but soon reassembled. Huddled together with wings folded, they watched and waited with a patience that sea and tides had taught them. Whatever happened, a banquet of young swan would ultimately be theirs.

Standing guard the cob moved back and forth, trumpeting now and again in answer to the anxious calls of his mate. Nothing to do but watch while the faint flutterings of the wounded cygnet grew weaker and finally

stilled. Not until the Arctic sun hung low and red did the hopeless vigil end, and the cob returned to his family waiting among the reeds.

In the weeks while the parent birds grew their new flight feathers, Olor went on trying out his strength. Though his own flight quills were not fully grown, he had learned to funnel upward and spiral down in widening arcs, bugling as he came. Already Olor could land in a spot scarcely larger than himself, a feat required of the mature swan who must often find space in a pond already crowded with waterfowl. He was half again the size of his sisters, who had become his faithful followers.

By this time the nestlings of all the other flocks had learned to fly and feed themselves, and the parent birds were enjoying an interval of rest. Trumpeter parents, too, were less vigilant. With flight feathers renewed they were once more socializing while this year's nestlings got acquainted. For a time Olor found special interest in some Canada geese. Sailing along with necks proudly arched, these might almost have been swans of a darker hue. Like the swans they reached underwater for their food, instead of diving for it in duck fashion. There were temperamental differences, however. Swans would share a meal, but when Olor sampled a tuber or two of a lot that the geese had come up with, the ganders came at him with necks outstretched, hissing and honking, even delivering a few blows with their beaks. Too surprised to be angry, Olor was pecked and harried right back to his own kind.

In this larger family of the flock, Olor encountered other strong ones like himself, and in the contest for wing power Olor was not always the winner. He tried harder, displaying before all his excellent spot-landing form, or he would come in with webbed feet extended like landing flaps, cutting a path in the water. He braced the breezes and glided. Once in a head-wind race with several other cygnets, Olor took advantage of a sudden uprush of warm air and shot up and up. Bugling with excitement, three of the other cygnets followed, but when the updraft ended they found themselves at an unfamiliar height.

Several anxious parents, including Olor's sire, had noted the reckless ascent of the cygnets, and there was anger as well as relief at their safe return. Several young necks were tweaked by parental bills. But to Olor's general zeal for flight, a striving for the heights had been added.

While there was scarcely any darkness and no particular temperature change, the legions of waterfowl lived in timeless enchantment. It was as if this northland's summer face would never change, yet all the time the birds were storing up the needed fats for autumn migration. Soon this added flight fuel would be needed, for the Arctic season was short.

By late August the wide reaches of the tundra turned briefly bronze, then back to dull brown. Clouds seemed to be waiting just over the northern horizon to drift lazily across the upper sky. They did not remain but in passing drained the sun of its brightness. Excitement began to fill the air. This furor was less urgent than springtime's fever-heat, but there was a sense of imminent change. Flock after flock rose from the waterways accompanied by their young, who now had to go into serious training for the long flight soon to come.

The niceties of flight formation were still to be learned; also matters such as the lift and fall created by the difference in air pressure above and below the wings, and always strict obedience to the signs and signals of flock leaders.

The trumpeters in their turn took to the air for long drill flights. Young birds fell into position according to the strength of their wings and automatically took their places in the triangle or the line. In long carries cygnets and the weaker flyers depended on the great wings of the lead birds to break the wind resistance. Instinctively the young birds learned how to ride the shifting air currents to save their own strength. Olor was a good apprentice, absorbing all that his elders could pass along. Particularly he watched and tried to emulate his father, who seemed to him the greatest and wisest of them all.

In September the smaller birds began to leave. Buntings and sandpipers, all low flyers, rose from the muskeg in tattered clouds without strict formation. A few of the hardier flocks tarried through the first fall cold. Mergansers and brants and Canada geese were still present in smaller numbers, and some of the cranes as well. A few of these would wait on the wisdom of the swans for final weather warnings.

The space and quiet the trumpeters had lacked in the spring was now theirs to enjoy. They hobnobbed, happy in the fullness of the year. Fall frosts were tolerable to thickly downed and feathered skins. Flight drills continued in a leisurely manner, the cygnets gaining needful experience. Especially now they must learn that endurance would be required of them. To Olor the growing sense of this was like a promise, for it meant that great adventure lay ahead.

Shell ice tinkled at pond margins. After the nearly endless days of summer, the southing sun seemed to race to its setting as if blown by the chilling winds. Light snow covered the tundra, and soon the lakes were frozen at their margins, though the deeper waters would remain open for a while longer.

Still no graceless haste marred the trumpeters' royal mein. They fed well, storing fat, and flock leaders watched the winds and read the signs. On a day of unnatural stillness with snow clouds gathering in the north, a sonorous rally call sounded and was answered by different family heads. The general signal was familiar from many practice flights, but Olor sensed a difference. This time it was the sign they had all been waiting for.

From numerous scattered groups the rousing sounds had come, but it was as a single flock that the trumpeters unfurled their great wings for the take-off, beating majestically away. The remaining ducks and geese were gone before that day's end.

Other life was still about. Snowy owls and foxes would remain. Arctic hares would survive the winter to come—those the foxes and owls did not catch. The lemmings would burrow deeper for their long winter sleep. But without the clamor of birds everywhere on land and waterways, the tundra was stark once more, a place of frozen treeless desolation stretching northward toward the Pole.

CHAPTER THREE

The Whining Airs

Mounting skyward, the trumpeter flock formed into two Vs of purest white, pointed south. The waterways had been strangely quiet, but a north wind awaited them above. There was flock talk before the lead birds directed the flight to a higher course. Here the prevailing wind swept them southward at near gale velocity. For the cygnets the buffeting was severe, and a few of them were blown out of line. These were counseled by their elders until they regained their positions and held them with stronger wing strokes and tightened feathers.

Olor's place was near the middle of the right arm of the forward V, his mother and sisters somewhat behind. His sire flew near the point, one of several lead birds ready to relieve each other at the head if fatigue or other problems arose. There was comparative ease in a rear position. Watching the first of the lead maneuvers Olor saw his sire move a bird or two nearer the point of the triangle. He watched his chance to follow suit, which came in a moment of crosswinds when the bird ahead of him seemed to falter. It took more strength than Olor had counted on to gain and maintain the new position, but he held it.

Later, when his sire took his turn in the lead position, Olor moved another bird forward in his own line. The young cob he replaced knew the error of this and overflew him, forcing Olor back into his old position. The resulting disturbance was noted by the lead birds and there were hoarse buglings of reproof, but the line was soon straightened again and the great wings beat a steady rhythm that sustained them all.

The ruby glow of an autumn sunset momentarily lit the flyers' white breasts; then abruptly darkness fell. Night passage was something new and unnatural to the cygnets. There were a few plaintive calls, answered by decisive horn notes from the elders: they were going on. Olor sensed but dimly the wide terrain spread out below. The sense of movement seemed diminished, as if he and all the flock were beating their wings in a vacuum. Low clouds hung across their course. Olor felt the raw cold of them. The thick vapors muffled the reassuring horn notes that were continually passed down the line from the lead birds. Later the flock emerged into the silvery light of a young moon. Once more the wide land was visible below them and stars shone above.

Olor was tired. Fatigue weighted his wings. This passage seemed to have been going on most of his life, and he was more and more afraid. His growing fear roused blood-memories of falling and being lost from the flock. When a downdraft dropped him through a hole in the air, Olor cried out like a doomed swan. Struggling mightily he was consoled to see that others of the flock were still about him, all caught in the same abrupt suction. Trumpeting notes from up ahead brought them into line again, and the flight swept on.

Olor was flagging. He was so near the end of his

strength that his exhaustion was greater than his fear. He must settle, he must rest!

But so, it seemed, must they all. A moment later sounded the signal to descend, and the triangle became a ragged line circling earthward. Olor smelled water.

The small lake on which they settled was a known stopover to the elders of the flock. It was in safe remote muskeg with good feeding along its margins—the seeds of pond lily and water-shield. Unguarded trumpetings and a happy gabble sounded as the flock skied in and shook and preened themselves after the long vigorous flight. All fed for a while, then settled to sleep. Olor snuggled as close to his great sire as he could squeeze, feather to feather.

The winds that had hastened their southward flight belled on in the high sky, but on the muskeg it was still and cold. Before dawn, ice had begun to form round the resting birds, and a few early risers were shivering with cold. Watching and waiting on the narrow shore were three Barren Ground wolves, gray white and glary-eyed like spirits of winter. Moored birds could become frozen in, a living banquet for the pack. This had happened before and the watchers were hopeful.

Olor woke to icy constriction at his breast and sides and saw six hungry yellow eyes. He had never before known the clamp of ice or seen wolves, but the danger was clear enough. He bugled sharply, rousing his sire, who thrust at the ice with his powerful neck and bill. Having freed his family, the old cob continued to chop a circle about his nearest neighbors.

As the cob chopped at the rim ice, two of the wolves made a sudden lunge and a cygnet in the shallows was snatched up. The rest of the flock floundered toward the lake's opposite side, where thick shoreward reeds offered

some protection. After scant feeding in the late dawn the flock resumed the southern passage.

In the next leg of the flight there was no north wind to push them along. The flock bucked a strong southwest breeze which slowed the pace and burdened the weaker flyers. More often than before the lead birds changed places, relieving each other. Olor observed this but did not try to follow their example. He was content to maintain his ordered place and learn the flight rules that kept the migrating flock in control. His inner ear keened to the signals that passed between the lead birds. For a time there seemed to be general indecision, for the calls back and forth had a note of question. At the same time the flight level was shifted, first lower, then higher, and again higher. The lead birds' signals continued.

Suddenly, magically, there was a change. It seemed that in these cloudy heights there were two rivers of wind flowing in opposite directions, and now they had discovered the one that was going their way. Ease of flight, even the comparative rest of long gliding on nearly motionless wings, was now theirs. It was as if something of the harmony of the great Quill Spirit had descended upon the flock.

Before the end of that day they were flying over a region of small lakes and stunted trees. The air had a tangy new scent of conifers that made Olor want to go right down there and stay. Such shaggy growth everywhere must mean feeding and shelter for them all. But the leaders pressed on. Sometime in the night there was flock talk, and the trumpeters began a wide spiraling descent. The chosen spot was a kind of slough where reeds and sedge made fair feeding for hungry travelers. Dwarf spruce and creeping juniper grew low to the ground, all bent and twisted by the ceaseless winds. Coarse caribou moss hung in gnarled beards from the low branches, delectable stuff with a sharp new taste.

The flock ate everything edible. The elders seemed to know this place. Low authoritative horn notes blended with the cygnets' cheerful flutings as the great birds fed and preened and finally rested through the night.

In the first light the swans were afoot in the scrub, wandering through the dwarf forest. They were cautious and unfamiliarly graceless on their large webbed feet, but walking seemed good, and they used their long necks to reach for the gray green tips of hanging moss. There were roots to eat as well, and leftover bits of leafage to be found under the trees. Coming upon a strip of familiar sphagnum moss, the cygnets settled to rest again, while their elders stood guard.

A strange noise roused Olor. It was a kind of clacking sound out of the depths of the scrub, as if heavy creatures were coming nearer and nearer. It seemed as if the elders should be alarmed, but they were calmly reaching for moss tips, paying no attention. Olor's mother likewise seemed oblivious.

The clacking sounds increased and at last heavy creatures did indeed appear, ten or twelve of them abreast in a column that seemed to have no end. They were tall and hairy and gaunt, with gray white beards that hung like the moss, and antlers like dead branches. The clacking sounds were made by their split-hoofed hairy feet as they passed in an endless file.

Olor stretched his neck to see all he could and those around him did the same, while the passing beasts turned their long gray brown faces to look at them. After a while

the young cobs began bugling with excitement, but the
passing herd never paused. It was the fall migration of the
Barren Ground caribou south to tree line, a phenomenon
which the older birds had witnessed many times before.
They passed in their thousands hour after hour. Long before the last of the column had gone by, the trumpeters
had turned back to the slough to feed again and had taken
to the air.

Now there were lakes and streams, the smell of them
on every updraft. More and more waters, finally one
that seemed blue and vast as an inland sea, but Olor's
excitement was blended with a sense of danger. The
leaders began directing the flight higher and away.

Abruptly the world below them seemed to explode,
and the air filled with the demon whines of bullets. A
terrifying invisible something clipped Olor's very wing
tip. In another burst white feathers scattered like snow
and the young cob who had overflown Olor that first day
was suddenly gone from his place. Olor saw him falling,
wings beating desperately to keep up with the flock. The
struggle ended. Motionless now he fell earthward.

The blasts from below continued to sound and the
air whined. Three more trumpeters dropped from the
pitching disordered ranks. Two of these were killed out-
right and plummeted to earth; the third, with a broken
wing, descended in a spiral to meet a crueler end below.

In Olor blood-knowing was so strong that it was as
if he himself had gone down with the fallen ones. He was
trembling, and his wings felt too heavy to support him.
Then clear authoritative notes sounded from the leaders,
bringing to order the disorganized ranks of the flyers,
and Olor steadied to the command.

CHAPTER FOUR

Endless Passage

In the next few days the strong-winged trumpeters overtook many flocks of smaller waterfowl which had left the Arctic before them. Along the familiar flyways, lakes and streams were crowded with ducks and Canada geese, taking it easy now that the worst of the cold was behind them. The swans, too, needed rest. They would have been glad to tarry a while with their old neighbors, but dangers seemed waiting for them in all the favorite stopping places. It was not men with guns alone that took toll of them; there were unseen mysterious enemies as well.

Again and again one of their number, having come to rest on a lakeshore or in the shallows, would be unable to rise again. He was held by the invisible strands of a man-made snare that could not be broken. Not even the wisest of the leaders could help the victim now, and the flock would have to leave with the snared one still crying out.

There was great terror in this. The young birds saw
that their leaders, too, were shaken, for always the flight
that followed had panic in it. Often they flew without
rest to some remoter spot, but everywhere, it seemed,
sharpshooters were waiting for them in the forests below.
Casualties meant tightening of the ranks.

Olor was experienced by this time in the tension
and fear that shook them all when without warning thun-
der burst from the peaceful-looking country below them.
But he had got past the feeling that he was one of the
fallen. After the shock of the blast from below there was
a forward surge. And when the leaders ordered them on
with compelling horn notes Olor's voice sounded with
theirs.

Besides the harassment of guns and snares, the flock
met the usual hazards of fog and wind. Storm drove them
off course into the Teton Mountains, and the exhausted
flock descended into strange new country. It was a wide
valley between towering white peaks with ponds and
lakes that steamed! They were afraid of these unnatural-
looking waters and huddled together on a shore. All
around them was new-fallen snow, and the storm wind
still belled in the peaks above, yet currents of warm air
came to them from the lake.

Suddenly the center of the lake erupted in a geyser
of steaming water. It was over in a moment or two, and
the lake was as before with clouds of steam resting upon
it. Now warm mists laved the trumpeters so pleasantly
that the bravest of them waded into the water. All
seemed well so the others followed. Floating, the swans
looked at each other through veils of mist, yet the temperature of the water seemed no warmer than a sunny

pond. Reassured, they fell to preening their feathers near the snowy shore. When the lake fountained again at its center there was a moment's fear, but the waters about them were as before and the steamy mist was welcome. After a time they found roots and tubers along the margin as in any summer pond. They fed and rested, and in the early darkness, moored together on the tempered lake, they slept.

In this high altitude winter had already come. Morning sun glinted on a crystal world of frozen slopes and snow-weighted pine boughs, and there was a glassy tinkle of icicles dropping from the nearby trees. Yet their lake remained warm and the periodic spouting of the geyser was no longer alarming. Olor and some of the other cygnets actually swam out toward the spot but retreated with excited flutings when the temperature of the water increased.

For a time there seemed no reason to be on their way. Days passed in this new habitat, and the tired flock recuperated, feeding and sleeping without fear. They flew to an adjoining lake, also open and warm, where the pine woods came down almost to the shore. Floating along beside their shadows the swans saw and were seen by a number of the woods dwellers. A wide-antlered moose stood for a long time with his forehoofs in the water, brooding over nothing. Finally he lifted his head and sent a hoarse bawling cry across the water. The sound was so loud and startling that several of the swans went into the air, but they soon settled again, for the cumbersome giant was just signaling a friend. He stood as before until an answering bawl came from the opposite shore; then he walked into the water and swam to the other side.

Once a black bear appeared in the woods shadows and ripped up a rotted log. A small band of elk stood on the shore and gazed at the swans with mild curiosity. All the animals seemed to go about their own concerns, never questioning the right of others to do the same.

In these Teton lakes fed by hot springs there would have been food for them and open water even after the temperatures dropped far below zero. But to the elders of the flock the urge south was a stronger lure than any present comfort or repose. Established migration patterns compelled them toward what had always been. After a few days the lead birds mustered the flock to flight.

In the period that followed there were few pauses. Often the lead birds would signal descent to some familiar stopover only to be driven up and away by sudden bursts of riflefire. Once two in succession of the well-known resting places had to be by-passed. When fatigue forced the flock down to a wooded creek near a settlement, dogs found them. The cobs managed to hold off the mongrels with hammerlike blows of their powerful black bills, but their masters had been roused by the clamor. Gunfire followed and three of their number were taken.

The rest of the flock sought hiding in the surrounding thickets—worming and squeezing, tight-winged, through brush and vines where neither men or dogs could follow—but it was long before their enemies were

lost behind them. Feathers torn by clutching briars, the
swans rested as best they could.

Southward again on this seemingly endless passage.

When at last warming airs brought a homing sense
of journey's end, a surge of joy swept the whole company. Ahead lay the lowlands and marshes of Louisiana.
At each familiar sign and scent, fresh trumpetings burst
forth. All new to Olor, yet it was as if he had always
known this place, and his excitement at arrival was almost more than he could bear.

The first gray of dawn had come as the flock descended in slow circles toward the home waters, a series
of marshy reed-grown ponds. Still in mid-air, their joyous
flutings ceased, and warning notes sounded. The circling
swans leveled off and lifted sharply, but not in time to
avoid the barrage of gunfire that broke from duck blinds
set up in the surrounding reeds.

The flock staggered and burst apart, then rising
formed again in a tattered line, their number once more
diminished. In shock and consternation an escape was
made, the shots from below continuing. In high sky, where
the rising sun shot flaming tints off their wide white wings,
the trumpeters circled for a final look at their old marsh
haven, which had become one more deathtrap for the
flock.

A resting place was finally found on an open sandy
shore. Then came the next order from the lead birds—to
head straight out across the Gulf of Mexico.

The trans-Gulf passage meant a five-hundred-mile
carry over salt water. It was years since the trumpeters
had made the Mexican passage, a time when their white

flocks had numbered in hundreds rather than in scores. Only the oldest of the leaders remembered those flights, but now it was hoped the old ways might save them.

All that day and part of the night the flight continued. Olor was a strong flyer now, but never since the first day of this long flight from the Arctic had he been so spent. He would sag with weariness, the wide waters seeming to rush up at him; then calls from the leaders would rouse him to fresh effort. Still nothing but water below. The flock alighted on it at last for a brief and foodless rest.

CHAPTER FIVE

Clock Of The Seasons

Morning, and below was a wild tangle of green with intermingled lakes. There was a vast shine of reflected light. Whole forests seemed growing out of the water and the lifting airs were warm.

Though all seemed well, the flock circled, calling. At one point below them there was a flash of white wings open and waving. Tentative trumpeting was answered by musical sounds from the water. Safety signals surely. A tremor of excitement passed along the winged line. Vibrating to the calls of his elders Olor loosed his own jubilance in a higher key.

The unhurried circling ended, and bird by bird the flock sailed in, the breeze of passage rustling their wings like wind through palm fronds. Their webbed feet braked them to a stop on the still, warmish water.

It was a family of whistler swans that had flagged them from below. As the trumpeters came in the whistlers set up their own special clamor of welcome. From the trees came the excited cries of parrots and toucans sounding off. Even before the amenities of greeting were over, the trumpeters were preening their flight feathers and rising on their webs to stretch tired wings. Olor had seized the stem of a tender water plant and was pulling it up inch by inch as he fed.

This tropical world was strange and unnatural to these visitors from the north. The warm humid air swathed and muffled them, and there were no keen rousing winds to launch into when they stretched their wings for brief flight. Driving rain widened the many small lakes till they all but flowed together as one. Sounds here were new and different, some of them savage and alarming, especially at night when dense bush along the lake shore came to throbbing, ticking, lethal life.

Instinctively the swans moored at the lake's center. Those that kept watch saw the shine of yellow eyes in the darkness, as death stalked there. Blood-hungry squalls sounded, and sometimes the cries of prey quickly cut short, and the cough of a jaguar. When the big cat had fed, the carrion birds came with piercing calls to pick at the remains.

For a time there were frequent alarms among the trumpeters, but they adjusted to the new environment. The sight of one another sailing beside their shadows composed them, and there was much of interest if they cared to look around. Now and again a pair of egrets flew out of the trees, wings slowly fanning, as if they were rowing through the heavy air, their long stick-like legs stretched out behind them. Frequent showers scarcely changed the temperature at all, for the tropical rains were warm. At the jungle's edge, hanging orchids were

so large that hummingbirds all but disappeared in them
as they dipped for nectar in the colored horns.

Missing their walkabout places in the muskeg, the
trumpeters discovered an islet of high ground in a neigh-
boring lake where they could waddle about and hobnob
with other birds. A pair of herons lived on the islet.
They were not particularly sociable, yet somehow com-
panionable as they stood eyeing the water, first on one
long leg, then the other. A resident tamandua helped
with the ant problem. He had a long sticky tongue which
he shot out from time to time, gathering up a large number of ants, his main diet. Sometimes a small band of
peccaries snuffled and squealed their way through the
bush. These were strong-smelling creatures that would
eat anything. When the swans heard them coming they
went quickly back into the water.

There was plentiful and varied feeding along the extended waterways, new lush roots and tubers and the
tender green leaves of half-submerged vines to snatch at
as they sailed along. Olor was growing fast. His first grayish coat was changing to one of flawless white, and his
already powerful neck had the proud arch of his kind.
His remaining sister—one had been lost during the long
southern flight—was smaller than he but a regal beauty.
Olor often squired her now, and some of the mock fights
he picked with other young swans were staged for her
benefit.

These were good-natured tussles but had the look of
serious combat. They were staged to impress the young
females, perhaps even the adult birds. Sailing at his sister's
side, Olor would give a sudden hoot at another male, then
splash him vigorously with his wings, peck at his neck,

and pull his tail feathers. Usually Olor won in these affairs, putting his opponent to flight, sometimes fastening onto his tail to be towed across the water. He might even sound off with a few trumpetings of victory before forgetting the whole thing to feed again.

Olor was in the midst of a sham battle one afternoon when his sister gave an unusual cry. Turning toward her he received a sharp blow on the neck from his opponent. Then his tail feathers were seized and Olor was obliged to tow the somewhat larger male to get to his sister's side. He was getting what he often gave, but his sister was in dire stress and the delay was costly. A brown water snake had thrown a coil round her submerged legs and was drawing her down.

At first Olor could not see what was happening, but when the attacker's tail flicked the surface he seized it in his bill. His head was pulled under water by the snake's contraction, and Olor saw the coil that held his sister's legs. He delivered a series of blows at it, which brought the snake's wedge-shaped head to the water's surface. Though it killed by constriction, it had not yet achieved its lethal second coil. Now Olor battered the creature's head, raining blows with all the strength of his powerful neck, until the snake had had enough and slid away into deep water.

Though this was a place of unending summer, the clock of the seasons ticked on and the trumpeters sensed the shift from winter into spring. In spite of humid warmth and jungle overripeness, high northing cries sounded from the cobs. With these differing horn notes came a mighty stretching of wings as if they were already in the

air. The pens responded with graceful flutterings and fussily groomed their flight quills. With their shapely necks elegantly curved, they nibbled and preened and waited.

The young birds were roused and excited. Olor especially made a nuisance of himself, imitating the cobs' travel cries, alighting with noisy splashes in the midst of his elders. Once his sire gave him a sharp pinch on the neck, but Olor continued to tail him closely. When the old cob glided toward his special marginal feeding place Olor was already there fluting peremptorily. The season had come for the spring migration. Olor knew it as well as if he had made the journey many times. The whistlers had already left and two families of trumpeters as well.

The old cob finally caught the excitement from his restless offspring.

The take-off was leisurely and casual, as if they were merely crossing to the island, but all knew that it was final and all were ready.

The flight across the Gulf was unhurried, but along the central flyway following the Mississippi their rhythm steadied and their speed increased. This trip the cygnets were comparatively mature—no need to regulate the pace to theirs—and ahead, urging them on, was the great spring breeding time in the north.

There was the confusion of fog over the river states, and bad weather met them above the Missouri River. Forced down on an isolated lake, the trumpeters found all manner of waterfowl riding out the storm, a gabbling, honking, whistling multitude. There was less danger from hunters in stormy weather, yet men found them the

second evening as the winds died down. It was a boat-
load of duck hunters, delighted to see swans among the
expected mergansers and teal, that fired into their midst.
The trumpeters lifted in panic, but two great birds
dropped back upon the water.

Perhaps the flock's clock of the seasons had been
ahead of time after all, for they were flying into winter
again. After the continuous warmth of tropical lakes,
the breath of the Canadian wilderness was chill. There
were stiff head winds to buck. Stretches of open country
below them were snow-covered, and the endless pine
forests were powdered with frost.

There were more losses to the flock in the airways
above the Great Lakes. On an evening of stormy red after an all-day flight, riflefire surprised the flock as it circled a pine-fringed inlet. The swans were still high, at the
top of what would have been their spiraling descent.
But the sportsmen below had special high-powered rifles,
and Olor's mother dropped from her place. Straight
down she pitched; then catching herself some fifty yards
below, her wings beat desperately as she strained to stay
aloft. In a moment her struggles ceased, and up to the
flyers came her plaintive cries, soon ended as she died in
the air.

The circle of swans straightened to form a wavering
line climbing toward the clouds. Far below, the fallen one
was visible on the water, wings outspread. The old cob
knew that his mate of the years had fallen. His voice
from aloft answered her cries, but flock law drove him on.
The flight was pressed skyward to escape the continued
fire.

For another night and day the leaders directed the flock onward without a stop. It happened that up beyond the tree line they saw again the brown flowing river of the caribou, returning in their thousands to the shore of the Arctic Sea. The herd's passage below, dependable as the return of spring, helped to make all things right again. Their next stop was a lake scarcely larger than a slough, but open and strangely warmer than the forest lakes to the south, because the north wind had given way to a western chinook.

Beyond this point there were no more hunters, and this year the trumpeters' arrival was early. Their chosen lake had wide stretches of open water, silvery soft in the muted light.

Olor's sire returned to his own point of land, the nesting place of so many years. Automatically he collected a few sticks and reeds but dropped them again before reaching the ruined nest. Sometimes his lonely call echoed over the water, or he would seem to be searching the skies for a flashing white form he knew. But he sought no new mate, nor ever would again.

The old cob's remoteness made it seem as if Olor had lost both his parents. Now he must grow up as fast as he could, but it would take years, for compared to other birds, swan maturity comes slowly.

CHAPTER SIX

Asa

That Arctic summer spent in the company of others his own age was followed by two similar seasons filled with adventure and learning for Olor, though they were years of great loss and vicissitude for his kind as a whole. Sportsmen now joined the hunters of the feather trade industry. Also the dramatically beautiful birds were in great demand for parks and private estates. Northern lakes and rivers were populous with other waterfowl, but trumpeter swans were increasingly rare. The same was true in the southern marshes where the swans had wintered.

Olor had now reached a size and wingspread equal to his sire's. He was a powerful creature with a zest for life and a great new interest in a flawlessly beautiful young female, Asa. With her he had often swum, flown, and fed before the moment of enchantment. But in this, his fourth Arctic summer, there suddenly seemed no other possible companion for him in all the white flock.

The thing was mutual. Not only did Olor seek her company at all times, but Asa sought his. After the briefest separation the two rushed together as if neither of them were complete without the other. Now their endless grooming and preening of feathers were for each other's eyes. When they gazed into the water it was not at their own image, but at each other's reflection mirrored there. Facing each other with spread wings quivering, they declared it all in the swan's beautiful courtship dance. Trembling and ecstatic, their bodies lifted and fell to a music that they alone could hear. Approaching each other slowly they touched breasts, then trumpeted happily and entwined their necks in tender embrace.

Yet it was still the prenuptial period that all trumpeters observed. While the older swans labored all day at nest building, egg laying, and feeding the young, Olor and Asa sailed about, basking, feeding, enjoying each other's company. If the day was warm they sought cool waters to float upon; if it was cool there was pleasurable warmth in the lee of every rock or tussock.

There was a narrow inlet between mossy reed-grown banks which they liked to visit. For some reason other birds did not come to this place, so the two had it to themselves. It was all one beautiful long day to them, for the sun went down the sky almost to the horizon, then rose again in an endless circle of light.

One pearl-colored morning with mist rising about them, Olor and Asa sailed into their secret inlet and took a long rest, necks entwined. Afterwards they were hungry and moved to the shallows to feed. Tubers and reed stems seemed richer here than elsewhere, the greens especially tender. Asa was feeding at the water's edge when a thicker part of the white mist detached itself from the reeds and advanced upon her. In the confusion of morning whiteness the Arctic fox had seized her before she could escape into the water. Asa gave one sharp cry, her wings beating frantically.

Olor, feeding at the water's edge a few yards away, came splashing toward the sudden tumult, neck outstretched, bugling a challenge. The fox's jaws had gripped Asa at the base of the neck. Flung backward, her wings beat the reeds and roiled the sludge. Her one weapon, her bill, struck futilely at her attacker's head, the blow sliding aside. She was being dragged into the thickets when Olor lanced in and his hard black bill went into action. One of the fox's rounded ears took the first blow; then with fiery wrath Olor struck at his eyes and muzzle, each unerring stroke driven by the elastic whip-like power of his long neck.

The jaw-hold upon Asa's neck was quickly broken, and she made for the water. For a short space the fox tried to meet Olor's attack, but the avenging swan was a terrible adversary. Confused and half-blinded, the fox gave up, melting back into the thickets.

Olor's head went high as he trumpeted his victory; then he joined Asa, who was waiting for him in the shallows. The two sailed out into broader waters and returned no more to the fox's range.

With the kingly formality of the swan kind, Olor's courtship of Asa was prolonged until another spring. His sire was gone by this time and his sister also, and only one of the former leaders remained to guide the flock. But as always the northland's magic beguiled the harried flock into vernal joy. Olor and Asa, in first rapture, were already looking for a nesting site. They considered the old parental place, vacant now and free to them on its well-chosen spit of land, but rejected it and sailed on dreamily, intent on some choice of their own.

Even though there were short happy flights of reconnaisance, Olor's surveys were farsighted. He marked a mossy inlet where ominous shadows moved in the crystal clear waters and noted as well a place in the muskeg where a pair of Arctic foxes had their den. There was an upthrust rock in the tundra where a gyrfalcon had his lookout. All enemies of the young.

It was from the air on one of their short flights that Olor saw the Place, site of their home to be, a cleared space on a bank close to the water's edge, high and dry and brush-free for yards around. The two staked claim to it with a few well-selected sticks and reed stems for the foundation of their nest.

There was no unseemly haste, but each day more sticks and reeds were added, to be laced through with caribou moss. The days were endless, the breezes gentle, and everywhere about them the land was greening. Arctic heather and the first wild flowers were coming into bloom.

Slowly the nest took on the proper shape and height, some four feet high and six feet across, pressed to roundness by the turning of their bodies. The final step was Asa's own—lining the cup of the nest with down plucked from her own breast. On that same day the first egg was laid, with three more to come.

It was not Olor's place to sit on the nest, but he was unfailingly attentive and patrolled the whole area with zeal, hissing steamily at anything that moved. Sometimes he brought her a present of fresh greens and fluted a solo while she fed. While Asa brooded, the pink saxifrage came into bloom. It was all round her so that in certain lights she sat in a frame of rose. Buttercups filled the hollows. The heightening sun stayed longer each day and seemed to radiate also from the four warm eggs beneath her breast.

Olor tried to see to it that Asa did not go too long without exercise. To tempt her forth he would lift into the air and settle close to the nest, then lift and settle again until her own wings involuntarily stretched for motion. Before leaving the nest Asa would cover the eggs with loose plants and stems. She would fly with him for a short way, and Olor would show her some fresh greens he had discovered. But these excursions were short. Asa's nerves and blood clocked the very moment when she should return to the nest.

One day she seemed reluctant to leave at all. Olor hung about coaxing and flexing his wings, and finally she stepped from the nest. Together they gathered saxifrage stems to cover the warm eggs, then flew across the water to a favorite bulb bed in the shallows. Abruptly, in the midst of feeding, Asa spread her wings for home. Olor followed in all haste.

From the air both of the mates saw what had called them back. Just slipping from the shoreward sedge was an Arctic fox making for the nest with small quick steps.

There were hoarse buglings as two winged javelins shot earthward. The hiss of air through flight feathers blended with the hiss of wrath from the outraged parents. At the last instant they braked their plunge. The fox had doubled backward but not in time to avoid the blows of two black bills that plucked chunks of fur from his back as he ran away.

While Asa settled upon the eggs, fussily adjusting

her wings, Olor stalked back and forth sounding angry staccato trumpetings that could be heard for a mile or so.

At long last two of the eggs cracked at once and soggy twins emerged. Then, quickly, two more eggs opened. Great excitement swept Olor. Asa's feelings were more contained. She housecleaned, gathering up each bit of broken shell, dropping it over the side. Then she warmed her offspring, and in the softest possible musical tones she made them know that though they had come out of the shell they were still contained in the protecting circle of the nest.

Olor, meanwhile, made several flights over the area, sounding forth his joy. He soared, descending in a spiral, skated for yards along the water, then sailed in again for a close check. All being well he stood at full height, wings outspread, and bugled triumphantly.

Now for both parents it was the great business of keeping the cygnets fed. Olor hunted while Asa waited at the nest, then it was her turn to hunt whatever crawled or wriggled among the stems. Snails too were offered. When the male twins and their sisters first entered the water, Asa's curved white neck and high-domed head hovered over the small foursome, guiding and protecting them. But soon they were on their own within nursery limits of the lake and were beginning to change over to a vegetable diet.

Flying lessons proved dangerous, for it was a strange summer. Predators abounded on the ground and in the air. Instead of one quick-stepping small-eared fox there were four foxes, and a small pack of Barren Ground wolves appeared from the south. Snowy owls were abroad even in bright sunlight, and from mid-air gyrfalcons watched, hovering and swooping. Skuas were always troublesome to the waterfowl but this year there were more of them.

The reason for this influx of predators did not at first appear, but it was not primarily to prey on the birds that these enemies had collected. There was a natural cyclic reason—it was a lemming year. For perhaps a decade the lemming numbers had been kept in check by the many animals that fed upon their kind. But suddenly the breeding habits of these small rodents got out of hand. Instead of the normal two litters a year there were four, and instead of the usual increase of four or five pups in a litter, there were six or eight. There were too many lemmings for their underground centers, so that they were crowded to the surface and began to overflow the land.

Now, suddenly, lemmings were everywhere. Themselves in search of food, they had become the easiest of prey, and hunters both winged and four-footed gathered for the feast.

In a curious way this lemming year aided the trumpeter pair in the safe rearing of their brood. There were always enemies, but while the lemming horde ran abroad, feeding was too easy for the predators to take issue with zealous swan parents for a trifling cygnet or two. The four young throve, surviving even the molting period of their elders, and were ready for flight when the first fall winds swept down from the north.

CHAPTER SEVEN

Olor and Asa

As a flock the trumpeters were now principally composed of cygnets, four from last year and seven from the two broods of the present season. A young and eager company, but a problem to the few older birds who knew the hazards of migratory flight and sensed instinctively the struggle to come.

This autumn in the north was unlike any other. Due to the lemming passage the land was picked clean of vegetation. Eating as they ran in search of more food and greater space for themselves and their progeny, and their progeny's progeny, the lemmings had devoured both leaf and lichen, tundra moss and tangled root.

For a brief time the land was alive with lemmings, a mass of small shapeless creatures on their way. On their way where? None knew. Perhaps right into the Polar Sea, pushed to their death by the pressure of their own numbers. Suddenly all were gone, and the predators likewise gone, for most of them accompanied the exodus.

As the year came to its annual pause at the edge of winter, the land was bare, but the lakes and flashets still provided food for waterfowl. Once again it was that electric time of change so full of exhilaration for the flocks. The cygnets felt it and celebrated with any and all of the fledged young. But the small group of adult trumpeter swans kept to themselves, seeming to treasure each others' company as in some final farewell. Olor and Asa sailed close together as in the days of their courtship, the very curve of their necks adding closeness, and their shadows on the water doubling all.

Once more no others existed. But only for a short time. For the young had to be coached and prepared for the perilous journey that was before them all. Once started, the drilling was severe. Like his sire Olor was a thorough disciplinarian. The drive that was in him reached far beyond his own four. His growing instinct for leadership would have included a large flock, if such there had been. The single old lead bird responded with lordly respect. There was no rivalry between the two, only a mutual dedication to the good of the flock.

Every lesson of prolonged flight was drilled over and over again. This was well, for the time came earlier than usual. All in a few hours the brooding desolation of winter spread over the already stripped and denuded land, and the trumpeter swans took their leave.

The Barren Ground passage was without incident; the cygnets performed with prowess, proving themselves equal to the passage. But a violent wind-stream from the west cut across their line of travel, sweeping the flock out across the broad waters of Lake Superior.

In the cloud and confusion of the storm all bearings were
lost. The flock pitched and floundered; every bird of
them, including Olor and the old leader, was pressed to
the limit just to battle through. The cries of two cygnets
beaten down by the wind were not even heard.

Exhausted after this ordeal, the flock was forced
down to rest in a wooded area patrolled by trappers, and
one of their number was snared. Olor and Asa found
each other in the scrub and kept close together through a
long night.

They were still off course as a result of the storm,
but in spite of all perils the urge was back to the familiar
flyways. At least the old lead bird felt no other pull and
drew the flock ever toward the central river states.
Though vaguely troubled Olor did not directly oppose.

There had been two days without undue stress, and
the flock was crossing a river when a barrage of four-
gauge shotguns shattered the quiet of a late afternoon.
Two young pens faltered in the flight. One of them,
fatally struck, fell with loosely flapping wings. The other
—Asa herself—sagged, then struggled frantically, calling aloud. She dropped a few hundred feet, held at
that level for a moment or two, then sank in a wobbling
arc toward a stretch of river woods.

Olor answered his mate with loud treble cries and
broke rank, but a sharp base note from the old leader
commanded him forward. Flock law, the habit of obedience, swept Olor on, but Asa had *called* him, and with
every wing-beat beyond the point where she had gone
down his own life seemed ebbing.

By the time the flock found a stopping place, on a
reed-grown river bank, it was not the fluting sounds of

the feeding birds that Olor heard but Asa's voice coming to him through the early darkness. Instinct stronger than all else was pulling him back. He swam apart toward open water, and almost of themselves his great wings quivered, spread, and had him in the air.

All the way Olor was calling. He knew instinctively when he had reached the stretch of river woods where Asa had gone down. In the light of a late rising moon he circled and circled, calling as before. No answer came, but a homing sense kept him hovering, his flute notes pitched lower as he dipped above the trees. With softest piping he let the silent one know that he had come.

On the water, a shallow margin with deep sedge, Olor too was silent, aquiver with listening. The answer did not come at once, but he was sure. What he finally heard, quite close at hand, was one thin low cry.

Asa had hidden herself in the thickest growth near the bank. There was no further sound as Olor pressed toward her through a curtain of standing stems, but there she was, and for a long time the two nestled close together.

Asa's right wing was injured and her breast feathers plowed by the spreading shot, but she had contrived to fall in the dense growth of rushes at the water's edge and had lain quiet, well hidden from the enemy. The search for her had been long and terrifying. Once the hunters had come within a few yards of her, beating the surrounding brush, but she remained motionless, and at last they passed on. When they returned, still searching, Asa had made herself as small as possible, her long neck back between her wings, bill tucked under. And finally they were really gone, the search given up.

Pressed close to her in the darkness, Olor sensed his mate's pain and terror and somehow took over for her so that she relaxed and rested. But this river woods was a place of danger. Morning might bring the beaters back again. In the deep quiet before dawn the two left their hiding place, swimming away downstream.

In the first daylight they sensed danger in the open water and hid again in the reeds. There was feeding in the shallows, and they lingered, swimming on again as darkness came. Though alone, without the prompting of the flock, the migratory urge still drove them, and their travel was south as the river flowed.

Sometimes in the night they heard high-winging flocks of waterfowl above the river and sent forth bugling signals that meant safe mooring. If the passing flock chose to settle, the trumpeter pair welcomed them, no matter what species of waterfowl they had called down. They were glad to feel part of a flock again and liked the babble of travel talk. After the tired visitors slept the swans continued to be happy in their company. Inevitably, when the time came for the stranger flock to take off, longing for flight seized them both. Olor's wings would stretch wide, then fold again. In hiding for the day, they would stay close together, flight quills touching.

There were times along the uninhabited swampy stretches when it seemed safe to move along by day and they made time. Sometimes they heard shooting or distant voices and were able to avoid trouble. In dawn and dusk, the hunters' hours, the only safety was in concealment. Earthbound days opened up a new and deeper in-

stinct for survival, especially in Olor. Often Asa seemed
weary of the long struggle, at the point of giving up.
Then he would lead her to cover in the shallows of the
stream and make low song while she fed.

Once after day-long travel they came upon a company of whistler swans moored for the night, and the
trumpeter pair was welcomed into the flock for an interval
of socializing and rest. Among these smaller relatives
Asa was as ever, tall and stately, gracious as a queen.
None noticed the crippled wing as she sailed happily
among them, part of the beautiful white flock. But
when the whistlers took off Asa gave a sharp cry and followed them at a splashing run across the water.

Olor went on quietly feeding in the shallows, waiting for her to rejoin him. In the wake of the whistlers
Asa had spread her wings. Abruptly she lifted in air,
alighting again half-turned about, after a short lopsided
flight. Regal and serene, she came sailing back to him.

It was a beginning. The injured wing needed much
strengthening, but it had healed. Caution and periods of
hiding were still a part of every day, but so were practice
flights. Like any cygnet Asa was learning to fly again, and
Olor was luring and prompting her with all the patience
of a parent cob. It was southern midwinter now, and
there were rains to sit out, but the urge southward was a
steady pull. By the time Asa could fly for an hour or two
at a stretch they had reached Louisiana and the bayou
country bordering the Gulf.

Then one evening as they flew together over marsh-
land waters rosy in the afterglow, there came a familiar
trumpeting from below. The two answered with glad

hoarse cries. Halting in mid-flight they turned, circling the area, and spiraled slowly downward while the calls from below became a full-throated song of welcome.

The company of trumpeter swans was small but they were their own kind, and Olor and Asa belonged. For the time, at least, the place they had come to was safe.

When once more the immemorial clock of the seasons struck the hour, and the cyclic urge was upon them, Asa was ready for extended flight, and Olor was spelling the two older cobs of the flock at the point of the small V. To the established lead birds spring flight meant the long passage north, and they headed for the old familiar flyways. But when Olor's turn came to lead the flock he veered far to the west of the river states and flew strongly, determinedly, not relinquishing the point of the triangle for hours at a time.

Olor was the largest, strongest flyer of the diminished flock, more than equal in his youth and power to the two older birds. More than that, dire experience not shared by others of his kind had prepared him for innovation and change. Having defied flock law for the sake of his wounded mate and then renounced flight itself to remain with her and see her through, he had learned great resourcefulness and a quality of vigilance which he would never lose. Now all his craft and guile worked for the flock.

Not that Olor knew what must be done to save them, but he was obeying a strong instinctual urge to find sanctuary for them all. He sensed the existence of a high mountain refuge where the enemy would rarely, if ever come. The image was clear—lakes and streams and tall trees. And peace. Somewhere in mountain country there was a safe place for them, and mountains were west.

Flock responsibility drove him, and the older birds must have sensed this, for after a while they stopped pressing toward the north, and all swept westward with mounting excitement.

The place of peace Olor sought was found at last in the Centennial Mountains of Montana, soon to be known as Red Rock Lakes Waterfowl Sanctuary, where the hunting of trumpeter swans would be outlawed and a refuge established. The Red Rock Lakes country perfectly filled the needs of the trumpeter swans. It was sufficiently remote, and there was an adequate food supply the year round as warm currents kept the waters open even in coldest wintertime. Olor's flock stayed, and in time other waterfowl found refuge there, too. Nests were built and eggs laid. The threat of extinction was lessened year by year.

Together Olor and Asa were a moving spirit in all this. As the flock had followed Olor west that spring, it now abided by his promptings to abandon the migratory habit of centuries and stay and thrive in their beautiful mountain sanctuary.

598
Ann
C. 1

Annixter, Jane

Trumpeter